Text copyright © 2003 by Lida Dijkstra
Illustration copyright © 2003 by Piet Grobler
Originally published by Lemniscaat b.v Rotterdam under the title *Muisje mijn Meisje*
Printed and bound in Belgium
All rights reserved
CIP data available
First U.S. edition

Lida Dijkstra • *illustrations by* Piet Grobler

little mouse

Front Street ⑧ Lemniscaat

L ong ago an old hermit lived on the banks of a stream.
One day, when he was resting in the meadow, an owl
flew overhead. Startled by the hermit, the owl dropped
the little mouse he had captured for his dinner.

The hermit jumped up and caught the little mouse in his cloak.

"Hello, Little Mouse," the hermit said. "You can stay with me, and I will take care of you as if you were my own daughter."

The years went by, and the man and the mouse lived peacefully in a cabin near the stream, gathering food, studying the stars and the moon, and playing with the animals.

But one day the hermit said, "Little Mouse, you are almost grown. Perhaps the time has come for you to choose a husband. Is there someone you would like to marry?"

"If I ever marry," Little Mouse said, "I would want to marry the strongest being on earth."

"The strongest?" the hermit asked.
"Who would that be?" He thought
and thought. Finally he said, "I have
an idea. Come along." And he took
her in his hand.

They climbed to the sun.

"Friend Sun," the hermit said, "you see the whole earth and you chase night and frost. You must be the strongest one of all."

"Thank you," said the sun, "but I am not the strongest. That big gray cloud can block my light. The cloud is stronger by far."

The hermit and Little Mouse went to the cloud.
"Friend Cloud," the hermit called, "you rule over
rain and drought. You must be the strongest one."
"I am strong," the cloud said, "but I am not the
strongest. When the wind blows, I'll be gone."

The hermit and Little Mouse struggled against the sharp wind to the place where it blew hardest.

"Friend Wind," the hermit called out, his hair blowing and his beard flapping, "you can uproot trees and throw ships against the cliffs. Surely you must be the strongest one."

"I have great strength," the wind said, "but even I cannot move the mountain."

So the hermit and Little Mouse climbed the mountain.

"Friend Mountain, you yield to no one," said the hermit. "Certainly you must be the strongest one."

"Ha ha," the mountain roared. "Me the strongest? What a joke. I am crumbling from a force that is stronger than all of us. Find him and you'll have found the strongest one."

"Who could be strong enough to bring
down a mountain?" Little Mouse said.

"Whoever it is must surely be the strongest,"
said the hermit. "We have come this far. Let's
go and see."

Trembling, they made their way into the mountain. After a
while they heard a noise, and around the next bend they found ...

… a mouse!

"Hello!" said the mouse. "Will you please move a bit?
You're blocking my light and I can't see where I'm digging."

"Friend Mouse," said the hermit, "*you* must be the
strongest being on earth! I'd like you to meet my daughter."

That very week the mice were married. They made their home in a cozy mouse house on the banks of the stream, and they stayed close to the hermit ...

... who, in the years that followed, welcomed many little mice into his life.